di

n

in the

snow

SIMON AND SCHUS
London   New York

When Miffy woke one morning

– just look at that, she cried.

There's been a fall of snow. Yippee!

Can I go outside?

The roofs look smooth and pretty.

The church is white with snow.

Don't worry, Mummy and Daddy,

I'll be careful how I go.

Miffy got her woolly hat

and wellies, right away.

With scarf and gloves she should be warm.

So off she went to play.

She rode her sledge right down the hill.

What a whizzy run!

As snow is soft as pillows,

even falling off is fun.

But when she put her skates on

to slide upon the ice

Miffy had to be quite brave.

An icy fall's not nice.

Next she made a snowman.

Up and up it rose.

Mummy brought a carrot out

to pop in for its nose!

Then Miffy saw a little bird

who had no place to go.

It tweeted, Miffy, it's so cold

out here in the snow.

Don't you have a home? she called.

You'll get so cold out here.

Then Miffy knew just what to do.

Yes, what a great idea!

Little Miffy went back home

for hammer, nails and wood.

I'll build a house for you, she said,

then did as best she could.

She banged and hammered all day long.

She made that house with care.

The bird looked oh so happy,

and warm and well in there.

What a lovely job you did,

Miffy's mummy cried.

But now it's nearly bedtime

so you'd better come inside.

Through the window Miffy gazed

before she hopped in bed.

See you in the morning, bird.

Goodnight. Sweet dreams, she said.

original title: nijntje in de sneeuw
Original text Dick Bruna © copyright Mercis Publishing bv, 1963
Illustrations Dick Bruna © copyright Mercis bv, 1963
This edition published in Great Britain in 2014 by Simon and Schuster UK Limited,
1st Floor, 222 Gray's Inn Road, London WC1X 8HB
Publication licensed by Mercis Publishing bv, Amsterdam
English translation by Tony Mitton, 2014
ISBN 978-1-4711-2085-5
Printed and bound by Sachsendruck Plauen GmbH, Germany
A CIP catalogue record for this book is available from the British Library upon request
10 9 8 7 6 5 4 3 2 1

www.simonandschuster.co.uk

MIX
From responsible
sources
FSC® C021195